Lee's Dad

hummingbird **rhinoceros** **grade**
hippo **Great Black Cockatoo**
Assistant Director **office**
bank teller **doctor**
giraffe **rules** **telephone**

1 Why did the children in Lee's class like their teacher?

2 Tell about the kinds of work the children's fathers did.

3 Why didn't Lee tell the class about his dad's job?

4 Name some animals the children saw at the zoo.

5 What does an Assistant Director of a zoo have to do?

6 Was Billy mean to Lee, or were the boys really friends? How do you know?

7 Do you think Lee changed a little at the end of the story? How?

Lee's Dad

by Norah Smaridge

Illustrated by

Phil Smith

The L. W. Singer Company, Inc.

A Subsidiary of Random House

NEW YORK • BRANDON, MISS. • DALLAS
DES PLAINES, ILL. • MENLO PARK, CALIF.

169.1 Manufactured in the United States of America 1A087
Library of Congress Catalog Card Number: 68-58305

Lee liked his new school.
The first grade was fun.
Today they had learned a song for Father's Day.

"Now we will talk about the kinds of work our fathers do," said Miss Clark.
"What does your father do, Billy?"

Billy said, "He's a doctor.
He makes you take pills, but I HATE pills."

"I spit them out," said Peter.

"But pills make you well,"
Miss Clark said.

"And what does your father do, Peter?"

"My father is a teller," Peter told her.

"What kinds of stories does he tell?"
asked Ana.

Peter laughed.
"He's not a story teller.
He's a bank teller.
He keeps your money for you."

"I don't want him to keep my money," Ana said.

"My dad gave me some money today.

He has a store.

He cleans things, and he takes out spots."

"Will he take the spots out of my dog?" asked Billy with a smile.

Everyone laughed.

Miss Clark turned to Lee.
"What does YOUR father do?" she asked.

Lee did not say.

Susan spoke up, "Lee never says anything.
He's a new boy."

Miss Clark smiled at Lee.

"Stand up," she told him.
"Nobody will bite you."

Lee smiled back.
He liked Miss Clark.
They all did.
She was fun.

"Well, Lee?" Miss Clark asked.

Lee stood up.

He said in a low voice, "My dad works in the zoo."

"I can't hear him," Ramón cried.

"Nobody can hear him!" Joan said.

"Speak up, Lee," Miss Clark said with a smile.
"We all want to hear you."

"MY DAD WORKS IN THE ZOO," Lee shouted.

Then he sat down fast—with a bump.

"In the zoo?" Ramón cried.
"Oh boy!"

"Oh boy, oh boy!" said Billy.

"That must be fun.
What does your father do in the zoo?"
Miss Clark asked.

Lee bit his lip.

"Is he a keeper?
Does he take care of the animals?"

Lee shook his head.

"I know," Billy said.
"He cleans the cages.
He pokes the lion to make him move."

"No, he brushes the monkey's hair," Susan giggled.

All the girls laughed.

"Quiet, please," Miss Clark said.
"Let Lee tell us."

But Lee shut his lips tight.

"Now Lee is mad at Billy and me," Susan said.

"And so am I," said Miss Clark. "You did not let Lee speak."

Just then the bell rang, and it was time to go home.

NO
PARKING

Lee ran out the door first.
Billy ran right after him.

"Hey, Lee," Billy called.
"Does your father REALLY work in the zoo?"

"Sure," said Lee.

"Tell me what he does," Billy said.

"NO," Lee answered.
"I can't tell you."

Billy made a face.
"I bet your dad does not work in the zoo.
I bet that's a big fat story."

Billy ran off down the street.

In school the next day, Miss Clark told the class they were going on a trip.

"On Monday we will go to the zoo," she said.

"Really?" asked the girls.

"Yippee!" shouted the boys.

"And maybe we'll see Lee's father," said Miss Clark.

"Where will he be, Lee?"

Lee bit his lip.

"I don't know," he said.

"I bet his father does NOT work in the zoo!" cried Billy.
"Lee is telling a big fat story!"

"BILLY!" cried Miss Clark.
"Lee does not tell stories.
Not even little skinny ones."

Everyone laughed.
Lee laughed too.
He poked Billy.
Billy poked him back.

"That's enough, boys," Miss Clark said.

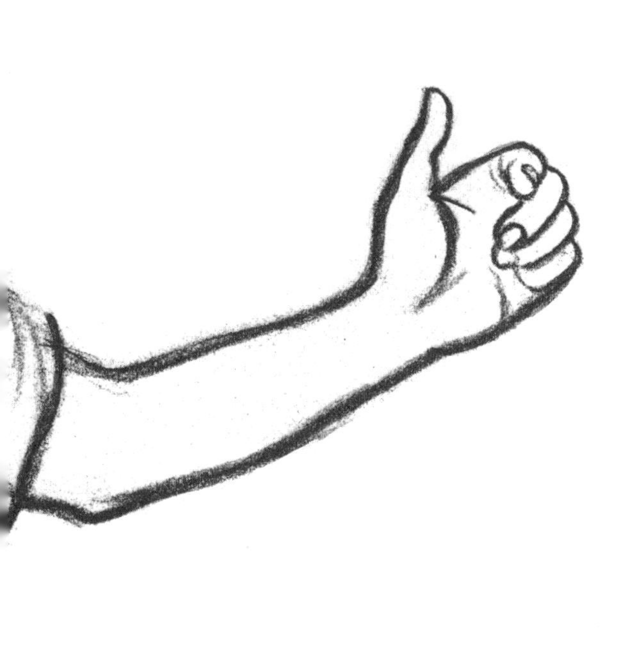

CAUTION
BUS

On Monday the class rode in the bus a long way.

They got out at a big park.

"This way to the zoo!" cried Sammy.

He ran ahead of the class down the path.

"Keep in line, children!" called Miss Clark.

When they came to the zoo, Susan said, "Let's go to the birdhouse first."

"No, let's see the monkeys," said Ramón.

"Let's buy balloons to pop!" cried Billy.

"We will go to the birdhouse first," Miss Clark told the class.

In the birdhouse, they saw many kinds of birds—lovebirds, sunbirds, hummingbirds, and a Great Black Cockatoo.

They saw a man put water in the cages.

"Is that your dad, Lee?" asked Billy.

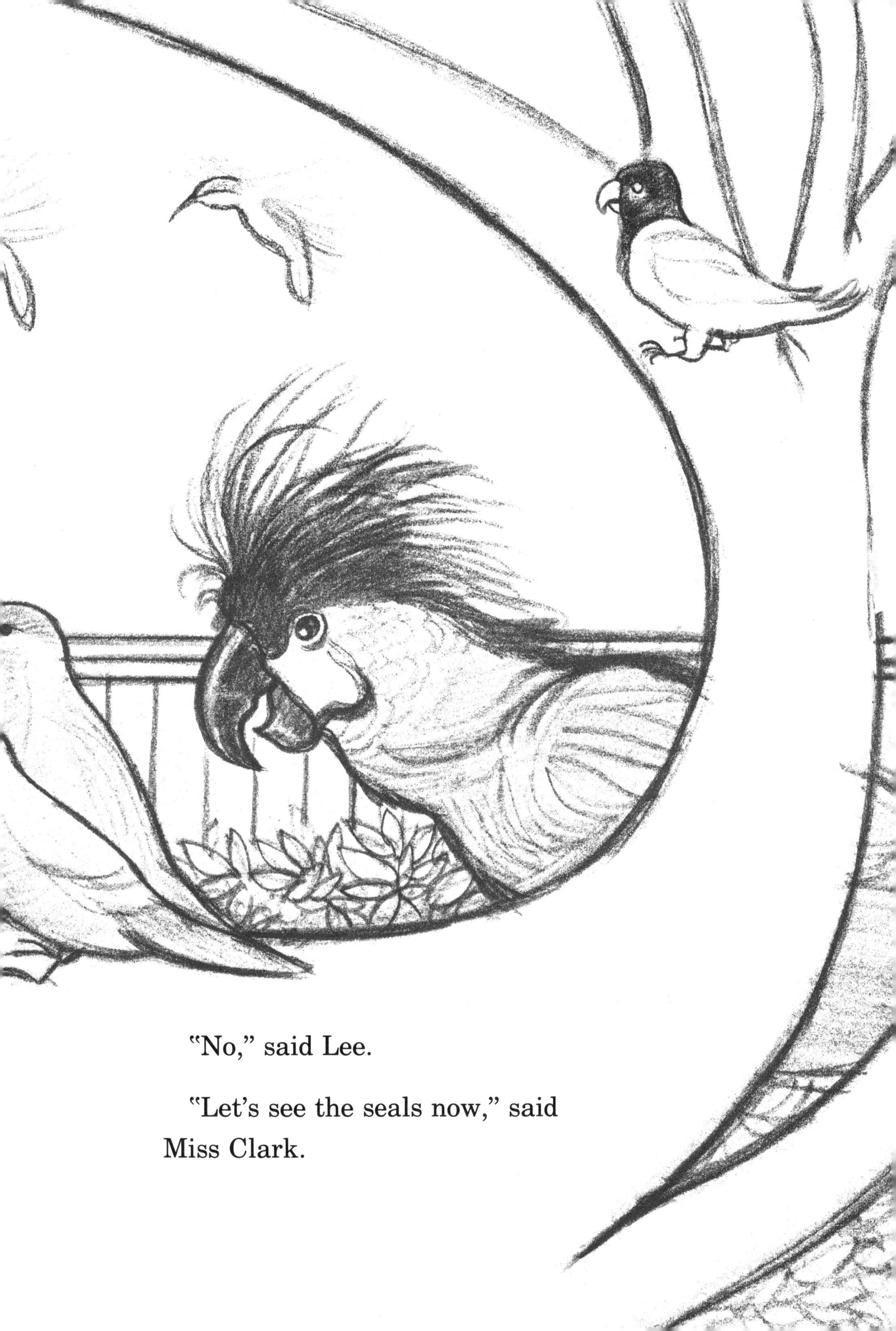

"No," said Lee.

"Let's see the seals now," said Miss Clark.

A keeper was feeding the seals fish.

"They make me hungry," Ramón said.

Sammy told Miss Clark, "Ramón wants a fish, Miss Clark!"

All the children laughed.
Miss Clark laughed.
Ramón laughed too.

Next they watched a man painting a shed.

"Is that your dad, Lee?" Peter asked.

"No," said Lee.

They saw a man brush a hippo's teeth.
They saw a man wash a giraffe.
They saw a man lead an elephant.
But none of the men was Lee's father.

KEEP·OUT

A man in the yard put some snakes into a box.

"EEK!" cried Ana.
"Is he your father, Lee?"

"No," said Lee.

"Now," Miss Clark told them, "we are going to see Lee's dad."

They came to a gate.
It said KEEP OUT.
They kept out.
But they peeked through the boards in the gate.

"But where IS he?" Ana cried.
"Do you know where he is, Miss Clark?"

Miss Clark smiled.

"Yes, Ana.
I know.
I called him on the telephone
before we came."

She asked a guard, "Will you please take us to Mr. Johnson?"

"Be glad to," the guard smiled.

The guard led them along the paths until they came to a big building. They stopped at an office.

A tall man got up from a desk.

"Good morning, Miss Clark," he said.
"Nice to see you. Hi, girls and boys!"

He smiled at Lee.

"Hi, Lee!"

"Hi, Dad," Lee said.
"This is my class."

"A very fine class," laughed Lee's father.

"Did you all see everything in the zoo?"

"Yes," said Billy.

"But what do YOU do here, Mr. Johnson?"

"Yes, WHAT?" cried the class.

Mr. Johnson smiled.

He said, "I help the big boss of the zoo."

"Lee's dad is called the Assistant Director," Miss Clark told the class.

"Yes," Lee said. "But I forgot that name.
It's too big for me."

"Come along, everyone," Mr. Johnson called.
"Miss Clark and I will lead the way."

Mr. Johnson opened a door that said KEEP OUT.

LOADING AREA

It led into a very big yard.
There was a truck in the yard.
One of the guards opened the back of the truck.
In the truck was a cage.

"You may come close.
But be very quiet," Mr. Johnson told the children.
"Sara is sleeping.
She is very tired.
She has had a long trip over the sea."

LION HOUSE

A big animal was on a bed of straw.

"It's a hippo!" Sammy cried.

"No," said Peter.
"It's a rhino!"

"Sara is a white rhinoceros,"
Mr. Johnson told them.
"The zoo has a white rhino called
Buster.
He was very lonely.
I had to buy Sara to be his mate."

"Will Buster like her face?"
asked Ana.
"She's not very pretty."

"Oh, but she is!" Mr. Johnson said.
"Sara is VERY pretty – for a rhino."

Mr. Johnson led the class across the yard to a cage.

In the cage were five little furry animals.

"Baby bears!" shouted Joan.
"I have a teddy bear at home.
He sleeps on my bed."

"Everyone loves bear cubs," said Mr. Johnson.
"The zoo didn't have any, so I had to buy some.
Now they are waiting for the vet.
He will see if they are well."

"Do you buy animals all day, Mr. Johnson?" Billy wanted to know.

Mr. Johnson laughed.

"Oh, no! I have lots of other jobs to do."

"Tell us about them," said Ana.

"Please," added Billy.

"Well," Mr. Johnson started.
"I make the rules.
I hire the keepers.
I buy the food.
I order new cages.
I take trips to other zoos."

"Mr. Johnson is a very busy man,"
said Miss Clark.
"So we must not keep him."

Mr. Johnson said good-bye to the children
as they left.

"Come back soon," he called after them.

The guard let them out, and soon
they were back in the park.

Lee poked Billy.
"You said I told a big fat story.
I'll bet you're sorry now!"

"I AM sorry," said Billy.

"Do you want some gum?" asked Lee.

"Yes," Billy said.

"Yes, WHAT?" asked Lee.
Just like Miss Clark.

"Yes, PLEASE," said Billy.

They both laughed. Lee took out his gum and gave Billy TWO sticks.